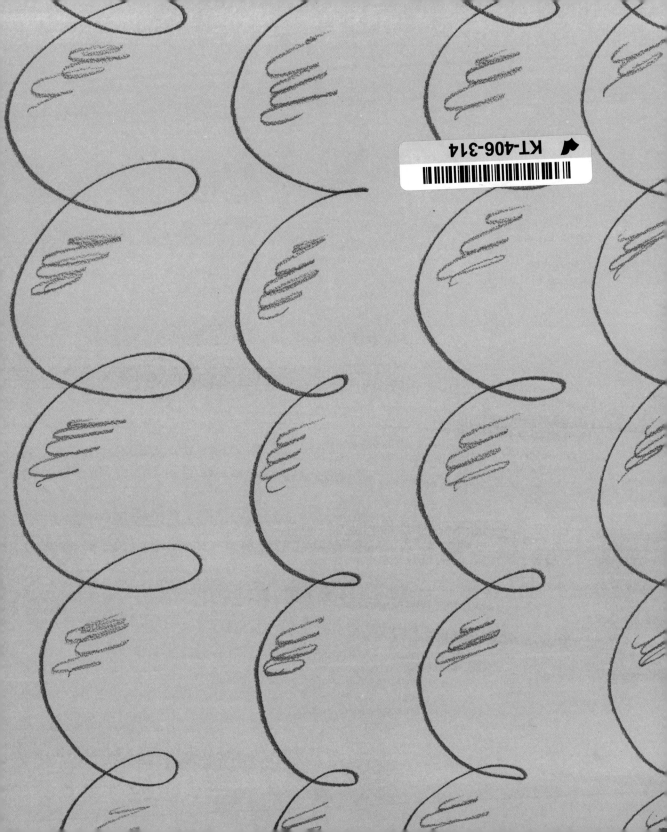

KT-406-314

Title
A Crocodile in My Pocket

Author and illustrator
Pato Mena

Linguistic advice and proofreading
Inma Callén

Publication
Apila Ediciones

Translation
Gerard McLaughlin

Printing
Ino Reproducciones (Zaragoza)

Binding
Tipolínea Encuadernación (Zaragoza)

First edition: **March 2021**
ISBN: **978-84-17028-47-3**
Legal Deposit: **Z 568-2021**

For the children of Buin.

I would like to thank Raquel and Eduardo, for trusting in this story and for putting so much love and professionalism into it.

Also Karina Cocq, for her valuable support and advice.

And especially Iolanda Marrasé, for walking by my side in this book. It would not be the work that it is without her encouragement and wise observations.

P.M

©Text and illustrations by Pato Mena, 2021
©Publication by Apila Editions, 2021

C/ Mosén Félix Lacambra, 36 B
50630 Alagón, Zaragoza, Spain

www.apilaediciones.com
apila@apilaediciones.com

All rights reserved

Any form of reproduction, distribution, public communication or transformation of this work can only be made with the authorisation of their owners, except as provided by law. Please contact CEDRO (Centro Español de Derechos Reprográficos, www.cedro.org) if you need to photocopy or scan a fragment of this work.

Pato Mena illustrated this book with manual and digital techniques.

This work has been published with the support of the Department of Education, Culture and Sport of the Government of Aragon.

A Crocodile
in My Pocket

Pato Mena

—Good morning, Tina! —says the newsagent—.
Why are you in such a hurry?

—**Because I have a crocodile in my pocket** —Tina replies without stopping.

—A crocodile?
Wow! Will you show it to me?

Tina then stops dead in her tracks
and answers her:

   —**This animal's bite has
the force of eighteen
hundred kilograms!**
**You want me to take it
out here, in the middle
of the street,
with all these children
and grandmothers?**

And Tina turns and
goes on her way.

A little further on she is greeted
by the fruit vendor:
—Hi, Tina! Why the rush?

—I have a crocodile in my
pocket.

—Oh, take him far away...
I don't want him to eat my apples!

Then Tina stops and answers him:

—You should know that crocodiles are carnivores, so before you worry about your fruit, you should worry about yourself!

And Tina turns and goes on her way.

A little further on, some friends say to her:

—Tina! Come and play, we need one more person!

—I can't now,
because I have a crocodile in my pocket!

—Woooow, a crocodile! —they all say, forgetting about the ball—.
We want to see it! Can you show it to us?

—OK. But just the tail.

—**Wow!** —they all say almost at the same time—.
How pretty!

Without further delay, Tina goes on her way.

And as she goes around the corner...
She sees her friend Bastian, waiting for her.

—Do you have your flamingo? —Tina asks.

—It's ready to go in my backpack.
What about your crocodile?

—It's in my pocket.
Do you fancy going to the park?
I think our animals would like to stretch
their legs before the trip.

—OK. Let's go!

When they get to the park, they find a quiet and pleasant spot by the pond. There, they watch their animals as they play and frolic among the leaves.

—Does your mom know
about the crocodile?

—No.
With so much work to do
and my little brother,
I don't want to cause her
any more worries.
What about your parents?

Yes, they helped me
with the flamingo.

—You know you can come
to my house whenever you want.
Plus, my mom makes
great cookies...

—Look! My crocodile
is eating your flamingo.

—Hmm... I'd say they're dancing happily.

—No, no, look carefully! Now it's swallowing it.

—You're right... but don't worry, flamingos always flock together, so I have more.

—How interesting. I didn't know that.

A little later the two friends and their animals continue on their way,
trying to go unnoticed by the adults and their pointless questions.

Until they get there.

—Nobody on this side.

—Nobody on this side either.

—Get everything ready, I'm getting the crocodile out.

After drawing the crocodile, Tina carefully folds the page and puts it in a different envelope from the one with Bastian's flamingo drawing (because no one would dream of putting a crocodile and flamingos together in the same envelope).

And without further ado they say goodbye.

—Have a good trip, crocodile!

—Have a good trip, flamingos!

Just before going into the classroom, Bastian dares to ask:

—What will we say to the teacher when she asks us about our favorite animals?

—We'll tell her that we did the homework, but that a classroom is not the right place for wild animals.

—And if it makes you feel better,
I'll also tell her that it was all my idea.

—But after school, let's go to your house
to eat those cookies your mom makes.

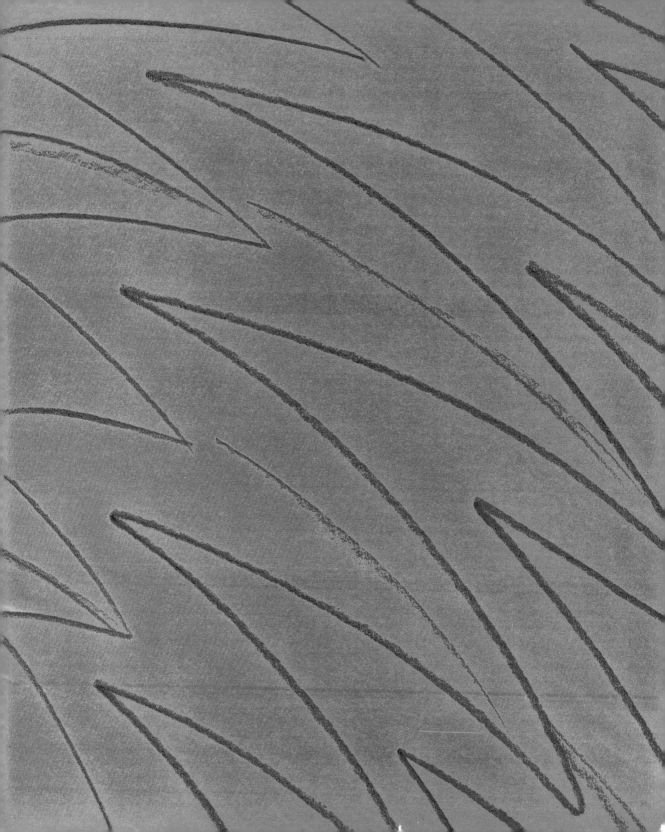